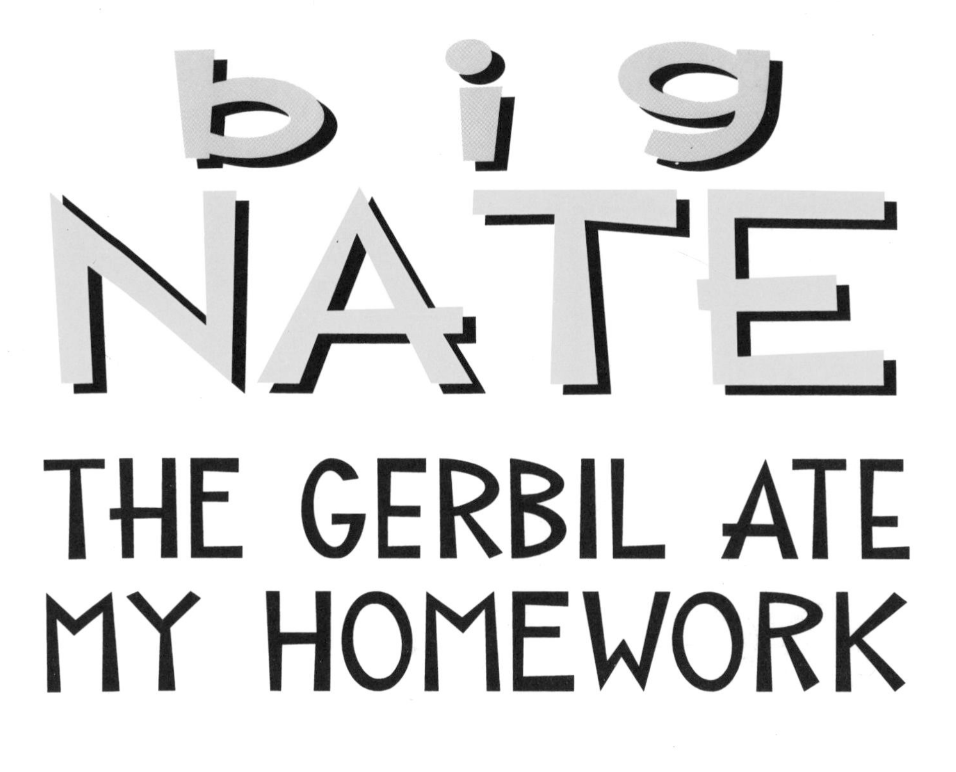
big
NATE
THE GERBIL ATE
MY HOMEWORK

Complete Your *Big Nate* Collection

big NATE

THE GERBIL ATE MY HOMEWORK

by LINCOLN PEIRCE

Andrews McMeel
PUBLISHING®

MR. ROSA! YOU'RE BACK!
I AM INDEED! HELLO, NATE!
OH, MAN! THAT WAS SO FREAKY WHEN WE WATCHED THEM PUT YOU IN THE AMBULANCE!
I MEAN, YOU'RE THE LAST TEACHER I'D WANT TO SEE WHEELED OUT OF SCHOOL ON A STRETCHER!
THE FIRST IS MRS. GODFREY, OBVIOUSLY. THE SECOND WOULD BEEEE...
LET'S STOP THERE, SHALL WE?
Peirce

SO WHAT **HAPPENED**, MR. ROSA? WHY DID YOU GO TO THE HOSPITAL?
I GOT DIZZY!
I WAS IN THE FACULTY LOUNGE, AND THE ROOM STARTED SPINNING! I WAS COMPLETELY DISORIENTED!
TURNS OUT THERE WAS SOMETHING WRONG WITH MY EARS!
YOUR EARS?
WHAT, THAT THEY'RE SO BIG?
NO.
Peirce

AN INNER EAR INFECTION?
YUP! AND IT LED TO A NASTY CASE OF VERTIGO!
I HAD ALL THE CLASSIC SYMPTOMS: I FELT SICK, DIZZY, AND FATIGUED. I HAD NO IDEA WHERE I WAS.
SO YOU CALL THAT VERTIGO, HUH?
UH-HUH!
WELL, MEDICAL TERMINOLOGY IS ALWAYS CHANGING.
I CALL IT SOCIAL STUDIES.
Peirce

OKAY, GANG, I KNOW YOU STARTED YOUR SELF-PORTRAITS WHILE I WAS OUT! WE'LL CONTINUE WITH THOSE TODAY!
YOU'VE ALL MADE SO MUCH PROGRESS!
SPLISH
SPLOOSH
SLOP
SLUP
SLOSH
SOME HAVE PROGRESSED FURTHER THAN OTHERS.
I COULDN'T GET MY HAIR RIGHT, SO I DECIDED TO PAINT SOME ZOMBIES!
Peirce

NATE, YOU ARE SUPPOSED TO BE DOING A SELF-PORTRAIT!
I KNOW. BUT I WASN'T FEELIN' IT.
DID VAN GOGH PAINT WHAT OTHER PEOPLE TOLD HIM TO PAINT? DID PICASSO?
UH... YOU'RE COMPARING YOURSELF TO TWO OF THE GREATEST ARTISTS OF ALL TIME.
YEAH.
THEY'RE THE ONLY ONES I COULD THINK OF.
I'VE MISSED THIS KID.
Peirce

...AND I LIKE THE BACK-GROUND.
MR. ROSA, IT'S YOUR FIRST DAY BACK. YOU MUST BE TIRED.
WELL... I AM A LITTLE BUSHED.
OF COURSE! YOU JUST GOT OVER A MAJOR ILLNESS!
YOU REST FOR A BIT. I'LL TAKE OVER YOUR ROLE OF DISPENSING CONSTRUCTIVE CRITICISM.
JEREMY, THAT PAINTING IS SORT OF A DUMPSTER FIRE.
WHAT A COMPLETELY INAPPROPRIATE IDEA.
Peirce

ARE YOU GUYS NUTS? THERE'S STILL SNOW ON THE GROUND!
JUST GETTIN' READY FOR THE SEASON, LUCAS!
WANNA PLAY? GO GET YOUR GLOVE!
NAH, I'M DONE WITH BASEBALL. I'M SWITCHING TO LACROSSE.
WHAT? WHY?
DUDE, LACROSSE IS MORE FUN!
BUT—
LUCAS! USE YOUR HEAD! THINK OF YOUR FUTURE!
MY FUTURE?
LET'S SAY YOU GROW UP TO PLAY PRO LACROSSE! THE TOP PLAYERS MAKE WHAT... FIFTY GRAND?
I DON'T REALLY KN—
AND LET'S SAY I GROW UP TO PLAY PRO BASEBALL, WHERE THE TOP GUYS EARN THIRTY MILLION!
DOESN'T MY FUTURE LOOK BETTER THAN YOURS?
NO, BECAUSE YOU'RE NOT GOOD ENOUGH TO PLAY PRO BASEBALL.
IT'S A LITTLE EARLY TO SAY THAT, DON'T YOU THINK?
IT'S 10:30. I'M OK WITH IT.

HI, MRS. CZERWICKI.
OH, DEAR. WHAT HAVE YOU DONE THIS TIME, NATE?
I DREW A PICTURE OF SATCHEL ON MY DESK DURING MATH.
WHAT KIND OF SATCHEL?
SATCHEL THE DOG! FROM "GET FUZZY"! THE COMIC STRIP!
OH, I NEVER READ COMIC STRIPS.
YOU KNOW THAT'S ABNORMAL, RIGHT?
EXCEPT THE JUMBLE! DOES THAT COUNT?
Peirce

YOU DON'T READ THE FUNNIES?
I'M AFRAID COMIC STRIPS JUST AREN'T FOR ME.
! !
WOW, MRS. CZERWICKI, WE'RE OPPOSITES! I READ EVERY SINGLE STRIP ON THE COMICS PAGE, EVEN THE LOUSY ONES!
WHY ON EARTH WOULD YOU READ SOMETHING YOU KNOW ISN'T GOOD?
...SAID THE WOMAN WHO'S HALFWAY THROUGH A ROMANCE NOVEL CALLED "TSUNAMI OF DESIRE."
IT'S FOR MY BOOK CLUB.
Peirce

Claudia didn't know which was pounding harder: the tropical surf or her heart. Lance, the ruggedly handsome lion tamer, had always been her catnip.

She gazed into his magnetic green eyes, which burned like two tennis balls beneath his auburn unibrow. Oh, how she'd missed him during the years he'd spent in the Congo, perfecting his perilous craft with the help of a pygmy Cat Whisperer.

I STILL CAN'T BELIEVE YOU DON'T READ THE COMICS! THEY'RE THE **FIRST** THING I READ IN THE NEWS-PAPER!
I GO COMICS, HOROSCOPE, SPORTS. THAT'S MY ROUTINE.
WHAT'S **YOUR** ROUTINE, MRS. CZERWICKI?
OBITUARIES, DEAR ABBY, AND THE JUMBLE.
OKAY, THAT'S SOLID. I CAN RESPECT THAT.
IF THERE'S SOMEBODY I KNOW IN THE OBIT-UARIES, I SKIP THE JUMBLE.
PEIRCE

WANNA HEAR SOMETHING UNBELIEVABLE? MRS. CZERWICKI NEVER READS COMIC STRIPS!
WHY IS THAT SO UNBELIEVABLE? I DON'T READ 'EM EITHER.
WAIT, WHAT?
BUT SHE HAS AN EXCUSE! SHE'S OLD! YOU'RE A KID! AND KIDS READ COMICS!
NOT ME. DON'T LIKE 'EM.
MRS. CZERWICKI, I'D LIKE TO REPORT A CRIME AGAINST HUMANITY.
WELL, THEN, HOW LUCKY THAT WE'RE ALREADY IN DETENTION.
Peirce

THIS IS RIDICULOUS! AM I THE ONLY PERSON IN THIS ROOM WHO READS THE FUNNIES?
I READ THE FUNNIES.
YES! CHESTER! MY MAN!
I READ "BETHANY."
CHUCKLE! YEAH, I READ THAT ONE, TOO, BECAUSE OF HOW LAME IT IS! IT'S SO STUPID! IT'S SO CHEESY!
I LIKE IT.
...AND UNDERRATED. VERY, VERY UNDERRATED.
Peirce

HOW'S THAT NICE GORDIE, ELLEN?
GREAT, GRAM!
THE TWO OF YOU HAVE BEEN TOGETHER QUITE AWHILE NOW!
UH-HUH!
MAYBE WE'LL END UP MARRIED SOMEDAY LIKE YOU AND GRAMPS!
IT'S POSSIBLE!
YOU'RE ABOUT THE SAME AGE **WE** WERE WHEN WE GOT TOGETHER!
REALLY? YOU MET IN HIGH SCHOOL?
WE SURE DID! I REMEMBER IT VIVIDLY!
IT WAS IN THE SCHOOL LIBRARY... THERE WAS A GROUP OF BOYS I DIDN'T KNOW SITTING AT A LARGE TABLE...
...AND YOU NOTICED GRAMPS RIGHT AWAY!
IT WOULD HAVE BEEN HARD **NOT** TO NOTICE HIM.
HE WAS THE ONLY ONE MAKING FART NOISES WITH HIS ARMPIT.
AND THE REST IS HISTORY.
SMOOTH, GRAMPS!
Ellen

READY FOR THE CARTOONING CLUB MEETING AFTER SCHOOL?
AM I **EVER!**
WHAT'S SO SPECIAL ABOUT TODAY'S MEETING?
MR. ROSA INVITED A **PROFESSIONAL** CARTOONIST TO COME TALK TO US!
YEAH, SHE'S WON A BUNCH OF AWARDS FOR HER GRAPHIC NOVELS!
HI, HANDSOME!
HEY, TRUDY!
I CAN'T WAIT TO GO ROLLER SKATING THIS AFTERNOON!
WHA-? YES! RIGHT!
TROUBLE IN PARADISE.

...AND WE'LL MEET EVERYONE AT "WACKY WHEELS" AT 3:30!
UH-HUH. GREAT.
YOU DO REMEMBER WE MADE PLANS TO ROLLER SKATE, RIGHT?
OF COURSE! HOW COULD I FORGET?
HOW COULD I FORGET?
NO IDEA. BUT I'M LOVING THE DRAMATIC TENSION!
Peirce

NUTS. WHY DID I AGREE TO ROLLER SKATE WITH TRUDY AND HER FRIENDS TODAY, OF ALL DAYS?
A REAL CARTOONIST IS VISITING THE CARTOONING CLUB, AND I WON'T BE THERE! I'M MISSING THE CHANCE OF A LIFETIME!
GUESS THERE'S NOTHING TO DO BUT MAKE THE BEST OF IT.
Peirce
WACKY WHEELS
"WHERE THE GOOD TIMES ROLL!"
SIGH...

WHAT SIZE SKATES, BOYS?
9.
8.
8½.
ENTALS
WHAT SIZE, SON?
6.
ENTALS
SNICKER! HEH HEH! 6!
THIS ISN'T A GOOD FIT.
Peirce

UT
Peirce

NATE! WHY WEREN'T YOU AT CARTOONING CLUB YESTERDAY?
OH, I WAS BUSY AFTER SCHOOL.
WELL, THE REST OF US WERE TREATED TO A GREAT PRESEN-TATION BY FAITH BLEEKER, A GIFTED GRAPHIC NOVELIST!
I'M SORRY YOU HAD TO MISS IT!
YEAH...
I'M MISSING A LOT OF STUFF LATELY.
Peirce

Time for...
Celebrity
INTERVIEW!
with BIFF BIFFWELL!
GREETINGS, friends! Today I'm chatting with the newest season... SPRING!
What's up, Biff?
WOW, Spring! You're YOUNGER than I thought you'd be!
chuckle! Well, I was just born yes-terday!
How's the job going so far?
GREAT! Almost everyone appreciates my WARMTH and SUNNY DISPOSITION!
Uh... you said "ALMOST everyone."
Right. The guy who had the job BEFORE me isn't too happy.
Who's that?
OLD MAN WINTER! He's in total denial that HIS time is OVER!
It's NOT over, punk! NOT YET!
Yes, it IS! Let it GO, dude!
NO! I'll show the world I've still got some LIFE left in me!
OH, COME ON!
Peirce

HEY! LUNCH LATER?
YEAH! SURE, TRUDY!
OKAY! SEE YOU AT OUR REGULAR TABLE!
UH... HOW ABOUT WE SIT SOME-WHERE ELSE TODAY?
YOU COULD COME SIT WITH ME AND SOME OTHER SIXTH GRADERS: FRANCIS, TEDDY, DEE DEE, CHAD...
WHAT FOR?
peirce

SO YOU WANT US TO EAT LUNCH WITH ALL YOUR FRIENDS?
YEAH! THEY'RE SUPER NICE!
I'M SURE THEY ARE, BUT... THEY'RE ALL SIXTH GRADERS! I'M IN SEVENTH!
NO OFFENSE, BUT WHY WOULD I HANG OUT WITH A BUNCH OF SIXTH GRADERS?
BECAUSE I ASKED YOU TO.
Peirce

THE WHOLE TIME WE'VE BEEN TOGETHER, TRUDY, WE'VE HUNG OUT WITH **YOUR** FRIENDS!
WE EAT LUNCH WITH THEM EVERY DAY!... WE GO TO THEIR PARTIES!... WE DO STUFF WITH THEM AFTER SCHOOL!
WHY CAN'T WE SPEND SOME TIME WITH **MY** FRIENDS?
I DON'T THINK I WANT TO.
Peirce

LOOK, NATE, I'M NEW HERE, REMEMBER? I'M STILL TRYING TO MAKE FRIENDS AND FIGURE OUT WHERE I FIT IN!
AND OBVIOUSLY, THE KIDS I'M TRYING TO FIT IN WITH ARE KIDS I'M AROUND ALL THE TIME! KIDS FROM MY OWN GRADE!
IT MAKES NO SENSE FOR ME TO SPEND TIME WITH SIXTH GRADERS! I NEED TO BUILD FRIEND-SHIPS WITH SEVENTH GRADERS!
OKAY.
YOU'D BETTER GET TO IT, THEN.
Peirce

NATE, WAIT! WHAT'S HAPPENING HERE?
WE'RE BREAKIN' UP, TRUDY.
BUT THAT'S STUPID! WE LIKE EACH OTHER!
YOU MIGHT THINK IT'S STUPID, BUT I DON'T.
I MISS MY FRIENDS! AND IF YOU WERE WILLING TO GET TO KNOW THEM, YOU'D SEE WHY!
SO LONG.
Peirce

TRUDY AND I JUST BROKE UP.
WHAT?
REALLY?
YEAH. AND I'M PRETTY BUMMED ABOUT IT.
HI, THERE.
BUT NOT TOO BUMMED.
YOU GONNA FINISH THAT BROWNIE?
peirce

MR. STAPLES, CAN I SKIP CLASS TODAY?
SKIP CLASS? WHY, NATE?
MY GIRLFRIEND AND I JUST SPLIT UP. I MEAN, IT LITERALLY JUST HAPPENED.
IT WAS PRETTY EMOTIONAL. I DON'T THINK I CAN... Y'KNOW... FOCUS ON MATH AND STUFF.
HM. I'M SORRY TO HEAR THAT.
...BECAUSE CLASS IS GOING TO BE EXTRA SPECIAL TODAY!
WE'RE GOING TO PLAY MATH JEOPARDY! WE'LL FORM TEAMS AND HAND OUT PRIZES TO THE WINNERS!
AND WE'LL HAVE SNACKS, TOO! I BROUGHT CHIPS AND SALSA, AND MRS. SHIPULSKI MADE SOME OF HER FAMOUS FUDGE!
IF YOU'RE TOO HEARTBROKEN TO JOIN IN, THOUGH, I'LL UNDERSTAND.
HEART-BROKEN. UH... YEAH.
...BUT I'M READY TO PICK UP THE PIECES AND LIVE AGAIN!
GLAD TO HEAR IT.
Peirce

SO HOW'D TRUDY DUMP YOU?
DID SHE LET YOU DOWN EASY?
WHAT? WHOA!
! ! !
TRUDY DIDN'T DUMP ME! I DUMPED HER!
RIIIIIIIGHT!
I DID!

WHY IS IT SO UN-BELIEVABLE THAT I'D BREAK UP WITH TRUDY?
IT JUST SEEMS MORE LIKELY THAT SHE'D DUMP YOU!
F
I MEAN, SHE'S A SEVENTH GRADER, SHE'S PRETTY, SHE'S SMART! AND YOU'RE...
F
YOU'RE... UM...
F
ACTUALLY, WHAT'S UNBELIEVABLE IS THAT SHE WAS GOING OUT WITH YOU IN THE FIRST PLACE!
HEARD THAT!
SIGH
Peirce

GUYS, IT'S **TRUE**! **I'M** THE ONE WHO BROKE UP WITH **TRUDY**, NOT THE OTHER WAY AROUND!

AND YOU KNOW **WHY**? BECAUSE I ACTUALLY **MISSED** YOU CLOWNS, THAT'S WHY!
WE'VE MISSED YOU, TOO.

I KNEW IT!
...BUT IT'S WEARING OFF QUICKLY!

IS IT TRUE? DID YOU AND TRUDY SPLIT UP?
YUP.
AW, I'M SORRY, NATE. YOU MUST BE HURTING.
THANKS, DEE DEE.
AHEM! PAY UP, CHAD.
RATS.
THE OVER/UNDER WAS SIX MONTHS.
I'VE BECOME A BETTING LINE.
$
Peirce

SO, DEE DEE... I GET THE FEELING YOU DIDN'T THINK TRUDY AND I WOULD LAST.
I HAD A HUNCH!
I'M **FABULOUS** AT SENSING OTHER PEOPLE'S EMOTIONS! I'M LIKE AN **EMPATH**!
AHA! AN **EMPATH**! LIKE COUNSELOR DEANNA TROI ON "STAR TREK: THE NEXT GENERATION"?
IF THAT'S AS DORKY AS IT SOUNDS, THEN NO.
NO, NO, TROI'S NOT DORKY. WESLEY CRUSHER IS DORKY.
Peirce

FESS UP, DEE DEE: HOW'D YOU KNOW THAT TRUDY AND I WOULD BREAK UP?
I **TOLD** YOU: I **SENSED** IT!
AFTER ALL, IT'S MY **JOB** TO CHANNEL PEOPLE'S BEHAVIOR AND EMOTIONS!
WAIT, WHATTA YA MEAN, IT'S YOUR JOB?
HEL**LO**? I'M AN **ACTRESS!**
...OR HAVE YOU FORGOTTEN MY SIZZLING PERFORMANCE AS MRS. POTTS IN THE DRAMA CLUB'S PRODUCTION OF "BEAUTY AND THE BEAST"?
I'VE TRIED, BUT NO.
Peirce

GRNNK GRNNK GRNNK
MRS. GODFREY, NATE'S GRINDING HIS TEETH AGAIN!
STOP IT, NATE.
I CAN'T!
EXCUSE ME?
I MEAN... I DON'T TRY TO GRIND MY TEETH! IT JUST HAPPENS!
NOISES DON'T "JUST HAPPEN."
THIS ONE DOES! I DON'T EVEN REALIZE I'M DOING IT!
SO YOU'RE CLAIMING YOU CAN'T CONTROL THE SOUNDS COMING OUT OF YOUR BODY?
YES!
WELL, THAT IS THE MOST RIDIC–
Beeeeyoww
AHEM. CARRY ON.
GRNNK GRNNK GRNNK GRNNK

I'M A BACHELOR AGAIN, MRS. CZERWICKI.
OH, DEAR. I'M SORRY TO HEAR THAT, NATE.
SE
YEAH. *SIGH...* I GUESS THE ROMANCE JUST RAN ITS COURSE.
WELL, IF THAT'S THE CASE, IT'S BETTER TO FIND OUT NOW...
ET
SE
... INSTEAD OF FORTY-EIGHT YEARS TOO LATE!
STRUCK A NERVE.
Peirce

GOING OUT WITH TRUDY WAS FUN, BUT I GOTTA ADMIT, THERE'S NOTHING LIKE BEING SINGLE!
IT'LL BE GOOD TO, Y'KNOW... GET BACK INTO CIRCU-LATION.
CIRCU-LATION. YES.
CIRCULATION IS KEY. LORD KNOWS, **MY** CIRCULATION ISN'T WHAT IT USED TO BE.
SOONER OR LATER, IT ALL COMES BACK TO HER VARICOSE VEINS.
MY LEGS LOOK LIKE A **ROAD ATLAS**!
Peirce

GOODNESS! LISTEN TO ME, RAMBLING ON ABOUT MY PROBLEMS! I'M SORRY, NATE!
THAT'S OKAY.
NO, IT'S NOT! YOU WERE TRYING TO TELL ME SOMETHING, AND I CHANGED THE SUBJECT TO MYSELF! PLEASE, CONTINUE!
WELL, I WAS JUST SAYING THAT MAYBE TRUDY AND I WEREN'T REALLY MEANT FOR EACH OTHER.
AH-HA! LIKE MY DAUGHTER AND HER NO-GOOD BOYFRIEND!
I COULD HAVE TOLD HER HE WAS A LOSER, BUT DID SHE ASK ME?
HEADING BACK TO MY DESK NOW.
Peirce

I WAS TRYING TO TALK WITH MRS. CZERWICKI TODAY, AND SHE KEPT MAKING IT ALL ABOUT HER!
HA! HOW IRONIC!
WHAT DO YOU MEAN?
THAT'S WHAT YOU DO! YOU'RE THE KING OF TALKING ABOUT YOURSELF!
WHAT? EXCUSE ME, BUT I'M NOT THE KING OF TALKING ABOUT MYSELF! I'M THE KING OF LOTS OF OTHER STUFF!
... LIKE CARTOONING, PRANK DAY, YO MAMA SMACK-DOWNS...
HE'S NOT TALKING ABOUT HIMSELF AGAIN.
SHOCKER.

HOW CAN YOU SAY THAT I ALWAYS TALK ABOUT MYSELF?
BECAUSE YOU DO!
LET'S DO A TEST!
GOOD IDEA, TEDDY! YEAH, LET'S HAVE A NON-NATE CONVERSATION!
Peirce
OKAY, HOW 'BOUT THIS: MY UNCLE PEDRO'S BUYING ME A NEW BASEBALL GLOVE THIS WEEKEND!
NICE!
SPEAKING OF BASE-BALL, REMEMBER THAT AMAZING CATCH I MADE LAST YE—
AH-HA!

YOU GUYS REALLY THINK I TALK ABOUT MYSELF A LOT?
ONLY ALL THE TIME!
HEH HEH!
OKAY, OKAY, MAYBE I DO. SORRY ABOUT THAT.
IT'S JUST... IT'S JUST THAT...
...YOU'RE SO DARN FASCINATING?
YES! JACKPOT!
Peirce

YES! THAT'S A FIVE!
UH... DAD?
PLUNK!
ON THE WAY HERE, YOU SAID YOU WERE GOING TO PLAY A LEGITIMATE ROUND OF GOLF TODAY.
YOU TOLD ME TO SPEAK UP IF I SAW YOU BREAK ANY RULES.
WELL, YOU HIT YOUR TEE SHOT FROM OUTSIDE THE TEE BOX. THAT'S A TWO-STROKE PENALTY. YOU ALSO HIT INTO THE WATER. THAT'S ANOTHER STROKE.
YOU MOVED SOME BRANCHES OUT OF THE WAY ON YOUR THIRD SHOT. THAT'S TWO MORE STROKES. PLUS ANOTHER STROKE FOR THE SECOND BALL YOU LOST.
SO INSTEAD OF FIVE, SHOULD I WRITE ELEVEN?
UH... YOU COULD.
...OR YOU COULD WRITE FIVE, AND WE COULD STOP FOR PIZZA ON THE WAY HOME.
A CADDY'S GOTTA DO WHAT A CADDY'S GOTTA DO.
THAT'S THE BEST I'VE PLAYED IN **AGES**!

JENNY! DID YOU HEAR NATE AND TRUDY BROKE UP?
OH, **NO**!
NOW HE'LL PROBABLY START CHASING AFTER **ME** AGAIN!
HI, DEE DEE.
YOU WERE SAYING?
"HI, **DEE DEE**"?
Peirce

AHEM! A LITTLE UPSET THAT NATE DIDN'T SAY HELLO TO YOU, JENNY?
WHY **WOULD** I BE?
IN CASE YOU'VE FORGOTTEN, DEE DEE, I'M GOING OUT WITH **ARTUR!** I DON'T LIKE NATE! I'VE **NEVER** LIKED NATE!
BUT YOU'VE ALWAYS **LOVED** THE FACT THAT **HE** LIKED **YOU**.
EW.
Peirce

LOOK, JENNY, ALL I'M SAYING IS THAT NATE WAS CRAZY ABOUT YOU FOR A REALLY LONG TIME!
...AND YOU GOT USED TO THAT! WHO DOESN'T ENJOY BEING TOLD HOW WONDERFUL THEY ARE?
I MEAN, WHEN PEOPLE TELL ME WHAT AN AMAZING ACTRESS I AM, I EAT IT UP!
... SAID THE GIRL WHO DIDN'T GET THE ROLE OF GOLDE IN "FIDDLER ON THE ROOF"!
EXCEPT NOBODY SAYS THAT.
Peirce

WANNA HEAR HOW I KNOW THAT TRUDY AND I WEREN'T MEANT TO BE TOGETHER?
IF I MUST.
BECAUSE I DON'T MISS HER! I'VE BOUNCED BACK LIKE A CHAMP! MEANWHILE, SHE IS SHATTERED!
NH
AND YET, SOMEHOW, SHE'S FOUND A WAY TO COPE!
OBVIOUSLY SHE'S IN DENIAL.
Peirce

Y'KNOW, EVEN THOUGH IT DIDN'T WORK OUT BETWEEN TRUDY AND ME, I STILL THINK DATING HER WAS A MAJOR POSITIVE!
HOW SO?
FROM A MATURITY STANDPOINT! GOING OUT WITH A SEVENTH GRADER TAUGHT ME HOW TO THINK AND ACT OLDER!
YES, NATE WRIGHT HAS GROWN UP!
SECONDS LATER...
HE HAS, HOWEVER, MAINTAINED HIS YOUTHFUL SENSE OF WONDER!
GREAT.
Peirce

KIM!
I HEARD YOU AND TRUDY BROKE UP.
SO I'M HERE TO OFFER YOU SOME CONSOLATION.
BUT REMEMBER, I'M ONLY DOING THIS AS A FRIEND.
TRY TO IGNORE THE OBVIOUS ANIMAL ATTRACTION BETWEEN US.
'KAY.
Peirce

COME AND GET 'EM!
COME AND GET WHAT?
HOMEMADE COOKIES! FRESH OUT OF THE OVEN!
UH... THEY DON'T SMELL LIKE COOKIES.
NOT LIKE ORDINARY COOKIES! THEY'RE MY OWN RECIPE!
FORGET HOW THEY SMELL! THEY TASTE FANTASTIC!
SHKK! SHKK!
KRRK! KRRK! KRRK!
CHONK CHONK CHONK CHONK
WHACK! WHACK! HACK! HACK!
I'LL TAKE YOUR WORD FOR IT.
"NONSTICK BAKEWARE"! HA!
Peirce

HOW COME NOBODY EVER CALLS YOU FRANK?
BECAUSE THAT'S NOT MY NAME.

YEAH, BUT PLENTY OF GUYS NAMED FRANCIS SHORTEN IT TO FRANK!
WELL, NOT ME!

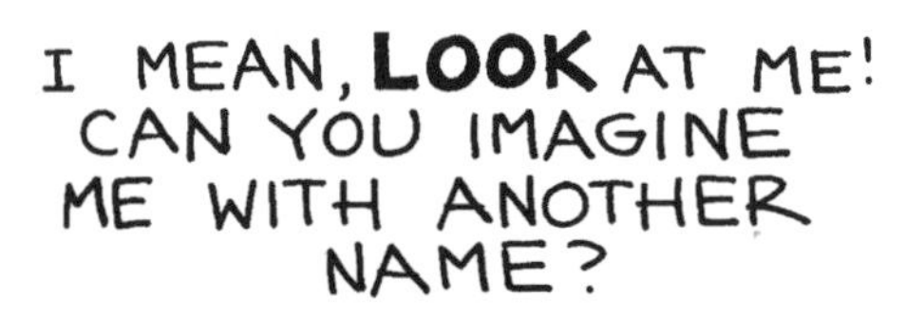
I MEAN, **LOOK** AT ME! CAN YOU IMAGINE ME WITH ANOTHER NAME?

MAY I SPEAK... HA HA!... FRANKLY?
SUDDENLY I CAN'T STOP THINKING ABOUT HOT DOGS.
YOU BOTH NEED TO CALM DOWN.

LET'S THINK OF A NEW NAME FOR FRANCIS!
WHAT? WAIT, WHY ARE WE DOING THIS?
BECAUSE YESTERDAY, YOU ASKED ME TO IMAGINE YOU WITH A DIFFERENT NAME! AND UNLIKE YOU, I'VE ACTUALLY GIVEN IT SOME THOUGHT!
BUT...
RELAX, I'M NOT GOING OUTSIDE YOUR COMFORT ZONE! I'M STICKING WITH BOYS' NAMES THAT SOUND LIKE GIRLS' NAMES! ASHLEY, SKYLAR, MICAH, CHRIS...
HOW 'BOUT LESLIE?
...OR LEZLIE! WITH A Z!
KILL ME NOW.
F
peirce

WE'RE BRAIN-STORMING NEW NAMES FOR FRANCIS!
NO, WE'RE NOT!
IT'S JUST FOR FUN, YOU NIMROD! DON'T YOU EVER THINK OF OTHER NAMES FOR YOURSELF?
I DO!
SEE? CHAD DOES! THAT'S THE SPIRIT, CHAD! WHAT'S YOUR ALTERNATE NAME?
TAD!
WHAT WE HAVE HERE IS A SERIOUS LACK OF IMAGINATION.
Peirce

WHY ARE YOU SO FOCUSED ON ME CHANGING MY NAME?
I'M NOT **FOCUSED** ON IT!...
I JUST THINK IT'S FUN TO SPECULATE ABOUT OTHER NAMES, THAT'S ALL! DIDN'T YOUR PARENTS CON-SIDER OTHER NAMES BESIDES FRANCIS?
HOW SHOULD **I** KNOW? I WASN'T EVEN **ALIVE** YET!
IF I HADN'T BEEN NATE, KNOW WHAT **I** WOULD HAVE BEEN?
QUIET?
NO, **ETHAN!** HOW WEIRD IS **THAT?**
Peirce

HERE'S A FUN GAME! WHAT THREE WORDS BEST DESCRIBE YOU?
OOH! I **LOVE** THIS KIND OF THING!
ATHLETIC! LOYAL! HILARIOUS!
MUSICAL! OPTIMISTIC! DRAMATIC!
1. BRILLIANT.
2. REBELLIOUS.
3. DANGEROUSLY SEXY.
THAT'S **FOUR** WORDS, PINHEAD.
SEE ITEM 2.
Peirce

MRS. GODFREY, A FEW OF US WERE PLAYING SORT OF A GAME EARLIER.
THE OBJECT IS TO COME UP WITH THREE WORDS THAT BEST DESCRIBE YOURSELF! BUT **ONLY** THREE WORDS!
1. SIT. 2. DOWN. 3. NOW.
THE LINE YOU'RE LOOKING FOR IS "OH, HOW I HATE HER."
THAT'LL WORK.
Peirce

HI, MR. EUSTIS.
HELLO, NATE! HOW WAS THE GAME?
STATE
COACH CALHOUN BENCHED ME.
OH, DEAR. WHAT HAPPENED?
STATE
I MISSED A FLY BALL.
REALLY? THAT DOESN'T SOUND FAIR.
LITTLE LEAGUE COACHES SHOULDN'T PUNISH KIDS FOR MAKING THE OCCASIONAL ERROR!
I'VE SEEN YOU PLAY! YOU'RE A GOOD OUTFIELDER!
IF YOU MISSED A FLY BALL, YOU MUST HAVE HAD A VERY GOOD REASON!
HE WAS WATCHING AN EPISODE OF "STAR TREK: THE NEXT GENERATION" ON HIS PHONE.
STATE
DURING THE GAME?
NOT JUST **ANY** EPISODE! IT WAS THE ONE WHERE CAP'N PICARD MEETS THE BABE FROM "X-MEN"!
Peirce

YOU'RE JUST STARTING THE HOMEWORK NOW? GODFREY'S ABOUT TO COLLECT IT!
I KNOW, I KNOW! I FORGOT ABOUT IT!
I'M NEVER GONNA FINISH IT! I NEED TO COME UP WITH A GOOD EXCUSE!...
...AND FAST.
SHERMAN! HELP ME!
NOW WHAT?
Peirce

WHAT ARE YOU DOING?
GERBILS SHRED PAPER, RIGHT?

SO ALL I HAVE TO DO IS... *AHEM!*... "ACCIDENTALLY" DROP MY UNFINISHED HOMEWORK IN SHERMAN'S CAGE!

WHOOPS!

YOU'RE ACTUALLY GOING THE "GERBIL ATE MY HOMEWORK" ROUTE?
CHEW! **CHEW!**
WHY DID IT GET DARK?

YES! IT'S WORKING! SHERMAN IS SHREDDING MY HOMEWORK!
GNAW GNAW GNAW GNAW GNAW
NOW I'LL SHOW THIS TO MRS. GODFREY AND SHE'LL HAVE NO CHOICE BUT TO GIVE ME AN EXTENSION!
GNAW GNAW GNAW GNAW GNAW
GNAW GNAW GNAW GNAW GNAW
HOW'S IT FEEL TO BE DRAWN INTO A TAWDRY WEB OF LIES AND DECEIT?
IT'S A LIVING.
Peirce

...AND THEN, I ABSENT-MINDEDLY PUT MY HOMEWORK ON THE EDGE OF SHERMAN'S CAGE!
UH-HUH...
IT MUST HAVE FALLEN IN! BY THE TIME I REALIZED IT, SHERMAN HAD TURNED MY COMPLETELY FINISHED HOMEWORK INTO A PILE OF CONFETTI!
AND WHAT WERE YOU DOING WHILE SHERMAN WAS DESTROYING YOUR PAPER?
UH... READING!
AND YET YOU STILL FOUND THE TIME TO STAND BY THE CAGE CHANTING "SHRED, SHRED, SHRED."
I WAS READING ALOUD.
Peirce

NATE, DID YOU ACTUALLY THINK I'D BELIEVE THIS ABSURD FAIRY TALE?
CONCOCTING SOME RIDICULOUS EXCUSE INVOLVING THE CLASS GERBIL IS MUCH WORSE THAN NOT DOING THE HOMEWORK IN THE FIRST PLACE!
I EXPECT MORE OF YOU.
YEAH. I EXPECT MORE OF ME, TOO.
GIVE ME FIVE MINUTES TO THINK UP A BETTER STORY.
Peirce

SORRY I MADE YOU PART OF MY LAME HOMEWORK SCHEME, SHERMAN.
I WASN'T TRYING TO GET YOU IN TROUBLE OR ANYTHING.
YEAH, I'D HATE GETTING IN TROUBLE.
THEN I MIGHT GET PUT IN SOME KIND OF **JAIL**.
THAT WAS IRONIC GERBIL HUMOR, BY THE WAY.
IT LOOKS LIKE HE'S SMILING BITTERLY.
Peirce

MRS. GODFREY, TAKE A LOOK AT THE KIDS FILING INTO YOUR CLASSROOM TODAY!
NOTICE HOW EXHAUSTED THEY ALL LOOK!
IT'S MAY! THE HOME STRETCH OF THE SCHOOL YEAR! WE'RE BEAT!
FOR EIGHT MONTHS WE'VE DONE NOTHING BUT LEARN FACTS AND MEMORIZE NAMES!
WE CAN'T ABSORB ANYTHING NEW! OUR BRAINS ARE TOO FULL!
TOO FULL? HM.
WE'D BETTER EMPTY THEM OUT, THEN!
POP QUIZ, FOLKS!
OH, HOW I DESPISE HER.
Peirce

HAVE YOU SEEN HOW MUCH MONEY THE LAST COUPLE "AVENGERS" MOVIES HAVE MADE?
A TON. SO?
SO... ALL WE HAVE TO DO IS INVENT A NEW SUPERHERO FRANCHISE, AND WE'LL BE RICH!
GOOD LUCK. ALL THE BEST SUPER-HEROES HAVE BEEN THOUGHT OF ALREADY.
...OR HAVE THEY?
Peirce

CHAD!
CHAD, I'VE GOT EXCITING NEWS!
I AM GOING TO MAKE YOU A STAR!
GAH!
IT'S A GOOD THING, CHAD.
SORRY. THOSE WERE THE EXACT WORDS MY GRAM USED WHEN SHE ENROLLED ME IN TAP CLASS.
Peirce

HERE'S THE SCOOP, CHAD: TEDDY AND I WANT TO MAKE A SUPERHERO MOVIE STARRING YOU!
ME?
BUT I'M NO SUPER-HERO! I'M NOT ALL MUSCLE-Y AND STUFF LIKE THAT!
THAT'S FINE!
YEAH, WE SEE YOU AS A NEW KIND OF HERO! ONE WHO DEPENDS NOT ON STRENGTH OR SPEED, BUT ON OTHER SKILLS!
BUT... THE ONLY SKILL I HAVE IS PLAYING THE OBOE!
WE CAN WORK WITH THAT.
TRUST US, CHAD. WE'RE FILM-MAKERS.

NOW THAT YOU'VE AGREED TO STAR IN OUR SUPERHERO MOVIE, CHAD, YOU'LL NEED A COSTUME!
OOH! I CAN HELP!
THERE'S A TON OF STUFF IN THE DRAMA CLUB STORAGE CLOSET! ANY TYPE OF COSTUME YOU COULD THINK OF!
COME ON, I'LL SHOW YOU!
THANKS, DEE DEE!
SOON...
WATCH OUT, BAD GUYS.
NOT WHAT WE'RE LOOKING FOR, CHAD.
BUT IT'S COMFY!
peirce

HOW'S THIS?
MUCH BETTER!
NOW THAT'S A SUPER-HERO!
LET'S START FILM-ING!
HOLD IT, WE STILL HAVE TO FIGURE OUT WHAT TO CALL HIM!
HOW 'BOUT LOSER BOY?
AW.
IGNORE HIM, DUDE.
WHEN WE WIN A PEOPLE'S CHOICE AWARD, WE'LL RIP HIM FROM THE PODIUM.
peirce

SAY HELLO TO THE WORLD'S MOST DYNAMIC NEW SUPERHERO! I GIVE YOU... MEGA-CHAD!
WHAT MAKES HIM DYNAMIC?
IF YOU'RE GOING TO MAKE A SUPERHERO MOVIE, SHOULDN'T HE HAVE SOME SORT OF... Y'KNOW... SPECIAL ABILITIES?
O.M.G! LOOK!
THAT IS ADORABLE!
I JUST WANT TO HUG YOU!
BEHOLD THE POWER OF MEGA-CHAD!
Peirce

IT WAS RIGHT HERE!
I'M SORRY, ANNA, I HAVEN'T SEEN YOUR NOTEBOOK.
BUT I HAVE!
MY NOTE-BOOK!
NATE WRIGHT, PRIVATE EYE, AT YOUR SERVICE!
HOW'D YOU FIND IT?
I SIMPLY USED MY POWERS OF DEDUCTIVE REASONING!
I OVERHEARD YOU SAYING YOUR NOTEBOOK WAS MISSING, SO I DID A THOROUGH SEARCH OF THE LIBRARY!
SOMEBODY OBVIOUSLY MOVED IT AS A JOKE! JUST A HARMLESS PRANK!
UH-HUH.
OR SOMEONE COULD HAVE TAKEN IT TO COPY MY HOMEWORK...
...AND LEFT CHEEZ DOODLE STAINS ON ALL THE PAGES!
THERE'S ENTIRELY TOO MUCH DEDUCTIVE REASONING GOING ON AROUND HERE.
TRAS

PRINCIPAL NICHOLS! WILL YOU BE IN OUR MOVIE?
MOVIE?
"THE ADVENTURES OF MEGA-CHAD"! I SEE YOU IN THE ROLE OF THE POLICE CHIEF!
YOU'LL PLAY AN OVER-WORKED ADMINISTRATOR, SLIGHTLY BURNED OUT AND STRESSED AS YOUR BELOVED CITY CRUMBLES AROUND YOU!
I THINK I CAN MANAGE THAT.
AND COULD YOU LOSE THE MUSTACHE? IT'S SO EIGHTIES.
Peirce

OKAY, LET'S REHEARSE! HERE ARE YOUR SCRIPTS, KIDS!
"YOU SUMMONED ME, CHIEF?"
"YES, MEGA-CHAD, I HAVE DISTURBING NEWS! THE EVIL..." UH...
POLICE CHIEF
NATE, ARE YOU BASING THE VILLAIN ON A REAL-LIFE PERSON?
WHATTA YA MEAN?
CHIEF
YOU'VE NAMED HER "MRS. GODSLEY, PSYCHOTIC SHE-DEVIL."
AND DO WE KNOW ANYONE WITH THAT NAME? **NO**!
CHIEF

I KNOW WHAT YOU'RE UP TO, NATE, AND YOU CAN PUT IT OUT OF YOUR MIND!
YOU WILL **NOT** CREATE A **MOVIE VILLAIN** BASED ON MRS. GODFREY!
OKAY, OKAY.
BUT "THE ADVENTURES OF MEGA-CHAD" NEEDS **SOME** SORT OF BAD GUY! WHERE CAN I FIND SOMEONE **EVIL** ENOUGH TO—
POINK!
Peirce

GINA? GINA! WANNA BE IN THE MOVIE TEDDY AND I ARE MAKING?
WHAT?
WHY WOULD I WANT TO BE IN YOUR STUPID MOVIE?
BECAUSE IT'S GOING TO BE AWESOME!
...AND YOU'LL HAVE A GREAT ROLE! AND... *AHEM!*... A GREAT CO-STAR!
CO-STAR? WHO?
CHAD!
KA SHWANG!

THE VILLAIN? YOU WANT ME TO PLAY THE VILLAIN?
YOU'LL BE VENOMA, MEGA-CHAD'S ARCHENEMY!
FORGET IT! I DON'T WANT TO BE SOME CRIMINAL!
GINA, THE VILLAIN IS ALWAYS THE JUICIEST ROLE!
PLUS, THE SCRIPT INCLUDES SOME ROMANTIC TENSION BETWEEN YOU AND MEGA-CHAD!
IT DOES?
IT DOES?
PEIRCE

WE'RE READY TO START SHOOTING! DEE DEE, WANNA BE IN OUR MOVIE?
I THOUGHT YOU'D NEVER ASK!
AHEM! WHAT ROLE DO YOU HAVE IN MIND?
OH, WE JUST NEED RANDOM PEOPLE. FOR CROWD SCENES.
WHA—? *GASP!* YOU WANT ME TO BE... AN EXTRA?
YEAH.
! !
HAVE YOU FORGOTTEN I'M THE PRESIDENT OF THE DRAMA CLUB??
YOU MAKE IT KIND OF HARD TO.
Peirce

PRINCIPAL NICHOLS?
HELLO, NATE! WHAT CAN I DO FOR YOU?
WELL... YOU KNOW HOW YOU'RE ALWAYS TELLING US WE CAN ACCOMPLISH ANYTHING IF WE TRY HARD ENOUGH?
DO YOU REALLY BELIEVE THAT?
I CERTAINLY DO!
I'VE SEEN IT HAPPEN COUNTLESS TIMES! WITH ENOUGH EFFORT, A KID CAN ACHIEVE ANYTHING!
ANYTHING?
ABSOLUTELY! THE KEY IS EFFORT, NATE! EFFORT BRINGS RESULTS!
OKAY, GOOD...
...'CAUSE MY DAD PACKED ME THIS LAME LUNCH, AND I HAVEN'T BEEN ABLE TO FIND ANYONE TO TRADE WITH ME.
I'VE TRIED EVERYONE.
EXCEPT YOU.
UH... WHAT IS THIS?
NO IDEA! SEE YA!
Peirce

"THE ADVENTURES OF MEGA-CHAD"! QUIET ON THE SET!
SCENE ONE: POLICE HEAD-QUARTERS! ACTION!
RRINNG!
POLICE CHIEF
HELLO?
CUT!
THAT WAS ALL WRONG.
PUMP THE BRAKES, BIG GUY. WE CAN'T ALL BE SUPERSTARS.
Peirce

I JUST GOT A CALL FROM THE STATE PENITENTIARY, MEGA-CHAD! THE EVIL **VENOMA** HAS ESCAPED!
EGAD! MY ARCH-ENEMY!
POLICE CHIEF
SHE BLAMES **ME** FOR SENDING HER TO PRISON! THERE'S NO TELLING HOW FAR SHE'LL GO TO... TO...
...UH... TO GET HER REVENGE... AND...
CUT! CHAD, WHAT'S WRONG?
MY LEOTARD IS GIVING ME A WEDGIE.
LET'S TAKE FIVE FOR A WARDROBE ADJUSTMENT.
Peirce

HOLD IT, GINA! YOU CAN'T WEAR YOUR GLASSES OVER YOUR MASK!
YEAH, VENOMA DOESN'T WEAR GLASSES!
BUT I CAN'T SEE WITHOUT 'EM!
DON'T WORRY ABOUT IT!
I'LL GIVE YOU DIRECTIONS FROM THE SIDELINES!
WHUMP!
LOOK OUT FOR THAT WALL!
Peirce

OKAY, GUYS, IN THIS SCENE, MEGA-CHAD AND VENOMA HAVE THEIR EPIC SHOWDOWN!
ANNNND... **ACTION!**
SO! VENOMA! YOU'RE UP TO YOUR OLD TRICKS AGAIN, I SEE!
YOU'RE ADORABLE.
CUT.
WELL, HE **IS**!
Peirce

YOU SEEM TO HAVE FORGOTTEN, VENOMA, THAT IT'S MY JOB TO PROTECT THE CITIZENS OF SLUMBER CITY!
CUT!
WOW. I SMELL OSCAR.
AN OSCAR? REALLY?
I WAS THAT GOOD?
NO, I MEAN I LITERALLY SMELL OSCAR.
THAT'S NASTY, OSCAR.
LUNCH MADE ME GASSY. SO SUE ME.
Peirce

SCENE TEN: CLIMACTIC DEATH STRUGGLE!
ACTION!
THE PEOPLE OF SLUMBER CITY ARE DOOMED, MEGA-CHAD! EVEN YOU CAN'T SAVE THEMMM...
...MMMMMMMMM...
!
DID YOU MISS THE PART WHERE I SAID "CLIMACTIC DEATH STRUGGLE"?
...MMMMM!
HELP!
Peirce

THAT DOES IT.
MYOW ROWR
HEE HEE
ROWR
WURF WURF
YOU'RE COMING WITH ME, SPITSY.
?
YOU'RE SPENDING WAY TOO MUCH TIME WITH CATS!
IT'S TIME FOR YOU TO BOND WITH OTHER DOGS AND LEARN ABOUT THE JOYS OF CANINE COMPANIONSHIP!
OKAY, WE'RE HERE! LOOK, SPITSY! DOGS EVERYWHERE!
NICNACK DOG PARK
DON'T BE NERVOUS! GO! HAVE FUN! PLAY!
WURF?
WURF? SNARRL! YIP! GRR!
GROWWL! YIP! YAP! *WHIMPER*
I CAN'T BELIEVE THIS.
NEITHER CAN I! PRISCILLA IS USUALLY AFRAID OF OTHER DOGS!

I'VE FINISHED THE EDITING! "THE ADVENTURES OF MEGA-CHAD" IS READY TO GO ON YOUTUBE!
YES!
NOW WE SIT BACK AND WAIT FOR THIS THING TO GO VIRAL!
AH...AH...
AH-CHOO!
...AND SPEAKING OF VIRAL...
SNRRK!
WIPE!
Peirce

RRRINNG!
YESSS!
FREE PERIOD!
LET'S HIT THE COMPUTER LAB!
YEAH! WE CAN SEE HOW MANY PEOPLE HAVE WATCHED OUR MOVIE ON YOUTUBE!
FOUR ISN'T A LOT.
ESPECIALLY SINCE WE'VE BOTH WATCHED IT TWICE ALREADY.
PEIRCE

... AND SO TEDDY AND I PUT OUR MOVIE ON YOUTUBE, BUT NOBODY'S WATCHING IT!
OH, DEAR. MAYBE I CAN HELP.
SURE, YOU COULD WATCH IT. THAT WOULD GIVE US **FIVE** VIEWS.
NO, I MEAN I COULD TWEET A LINK TO YOUR MOVIE!
WHA-? MRS. SHIPULSKI, YOU'RE ON TWITTER?
I HAVE 22 MILLION FOLLOW-ERS.
22 M-M-M-M-MUH-MUH-MIL... MILLION...
IS THAT GOOD?
Peirce

MRS. SHIPULSKI! YOU HAVE **22 MILLION** TWITTER FOLLOWERS?
UH-HUH!

I TWEET ABOUT ALL **KINDS** OF THINGS!
BUT THAT'S... IT JUST SEEMS **IM-POSSIBLE!**

I MEAN, TWITTER'S TOP 100 MOST FOL-LOWED PEOPLE ARE **FAMOUS!** LIKE KATY PERRY AND TAYLOR SWIFT AND...

...AND GERALDINE SHIPULSKI.
OOH! I'VE PASSED PITBULL!
Peirce

MRS. SHIPULSKI, YOU HAVE SO MANY TWITTER FOLLOWERS, IT'S INSANE! YOU'RE A CELEBRITY!
OH, PSHAW!
I'M NO CELEBRITY! I'M JUST A SCHOOL SECRETARY WHO TWEETS ABOUT MY JOB, MY FAMILY, MY BOOK CLUB...
YEAH, BUT LOOK! ALL THESE FAMOUS PEOPLE ARE YOUR FANS!
SNOOP DOGG WANTS TO PARTY WITH YOU.
NO CAN DO. I'M A CAT PERSON.
Peirce

I CAN'T BELIEVE MRS. SHIPULSKI, OF ALL PEOPLE, IS A TWITTER SENSATION!
I'M GONNA CHECK OUT HER FEED.

WOW! LOOK AT ALL THESE TWEETS AND RETWEETS! THERE'S **DOZENS** OF 'EM! JUST FROM **TODAY**!

WHERE DOES SHE FIND THE TIME TO DO HER **JOB**?

MEANWHILE...
DON'T YOU HAVE SOME FILING TO DO?
AT SOME POINT.
TICKA TICKA TICKA TICKA TICKA
Peirce

RRRRINNG!!
BEFORE YOU LEAVE, PEOPLE, HAND IN YOUR HOMEWORK!
HERE, MR. GALVIN.
GOOD GRAVY! NOT AGAIN!
NATE, I'M TIRED OF YOU HANDING IN WORK THAT'S COVERED IN FOOD STAINS!
GREASE! CHOCOLATE! SODA! KETCHUP! THERE'S NO EXCUSE FOR THIS MESS!
WHEN I RETURN THIS TO YOU TOMORROW, YOU'LL SEE THAT I'VE DEDUCTED TEN POINTS FROM YOUR SCORE... FOR SLOPPINESS!
MAYBE THAT'LL TEACH HIM NOT TO—
ARRGH!
KLUNK!
SPLOOSH!
MY COFFEE GOT ALL OVER...
DRIP
DRIP
DRIP
DRIP
DRIP
NEXT DAY...
MY DOG ATE YOUR HOMEWORK.
Peirce

OH, NO. HERE COMES WHITEY.
WHY "OH, NO"?

BECAUSE, DEE DEE, HE'S GOING TO GIVE US T'SUP HUGS!
SO? I LIKE HIS T'SUP HUGS!

T'SUP?

KRAK!

WOO! MY BACK FEELS SO MUCH BETTER!
T'SUP?
MY BACK'S FINE.

T'SUP?
OOF!
HOW COME YOU'RE SO INTO HUGS, WHITEY?
IT'S JUST MY JAM, DUDE! I HUG EVERYONE!
EVERYONE?
EVERY-ONE!
EVEN HIM?
ULP!
Peirce

YOU... YOU WANT ME TO HUG HIM?
HEY, YOU JUST CLAIMED YOU HUG EVERYONE!
YEAH, BUT—
NO STALLING, WHITEY! TIME TO GET THIS PARTY STARTED!
YO! CHESTER! WHITEY WANTS TO SEE YOU!
STOMP!... STOMP!... STOMP!... STOMP!... STOMP!...
TIME TO PUT YOUR HUGS WHERE YOUR MOUTH IS.

WHAT DO YOU WANT?
UM... HI, CHESTER... I JUST... UH... WANTED TO SAY...
...T'SUP?
CRUNCH!
I DON'T LIKE WHEN PEOPLE TOUCH ME.
I'LL KEEP THAT IN MIND.
NICE TRY, WHITEY!
TRASH
Peirce

WHAT HAPPENED?
YOUR BOYFRIEND, THAT'S WHAT HAPPENED!
HEH HEH!
RASH
WHITEY TRIED TO GIVE CHESTER A T'SUP HUG, AND CHESTER WENT OFF!
AW. SORRY THAT HAPPENED.
THANKS, KIM.
LET ME COMFORT YOU.
NO, HIM! COMFORT HIM!!

KIM, KNOCK IT OFF! STOP TRYING TO HUG ME!
GO HUG CHESTER! HE'S YOUR BOYFRIEND!
EXACTLY. I LIKE MAKING HIM JEALOUS.
WELL, THERE'S GOT TO BE A BETTER WAY OF MAKING HIM JEALOUS THAN HUGGING ME!
HM. YOU'RE RIGHT.
PUCKER UP.
NO!
Peirce

AFTER WE WARM UP, I WANT TO PRACTICE MY SLIDER!
YOUR SLIDER?
WHAT DO YOU NEED A SLIDER FOR? YOU'RE AN OUTFIELDER!
MOST OF THE TIME, YEAH!
BUT WHAT IF COACH BRINGS ME IN AS A RELIEF PITCHER?
A SLIDER WILL COMPLEMENT MY KILLER FASTBALL!
KIDS OUR AGE AREN'T SUPPOSED TO THROW BREAK-ING BALLS!
THEY PUT TOO MUCH STRESS ON YOUR ARM!
WHAT ARE WE TALKING ABOUT?
SLIDERS, CHAD.
OOH! YUM!
THE ONES DOWN AT "BURGER BARN" ARE AWESOME!
JUMBO PLATE OF SLIDERS?
RIGHT HERE!
NICE PITCH, CHAD!

TO PREPARE YOURSELF FOR THE FINAL EXAM, NATE, I WANT YOU TO JOIN A STUDY GROUP.
RESEARCH INDICATES THAT MOST STUDENTS BENEFIT FROM WORKING IN TEAMS.
AH-HA! MOST STUDENTS! BUT NOT ALL!
HAS IT EVER OCCURRED TO YOU, MRS. GODFREY, THAT I'M NOT LIKE "MOST STUDENTS"?
IT OCCURS TO ME PRETTY MUCH ON A DAILY BASIS.
I'M MORE OF A "LONE WOLF" TYPE.
Peirce

LIAM... ZOEY... NATE WILL BE JOINING YOUR STUDY GROUP.
WAIT, WHAT?
WHY DO I HAVE TO STUDY WITH THEM? WHY CAN'T I STUDY WITH FRANCIS AND TEDDY?
I CRAMMED FOR THE MIDTERM WITH THOSE GUYS AND IT WENT FINE!
"FINE"?
YOU GOT A C, TEDDY GOT A C PLUS, AND FRANCIS GOT P.T.S.D!
I'M SCARED.
Peirce

GRUMBLE LOOKS LIKE WE'RE STUDYING TOGETHER.
UH... OKAY, LET'S GO OVER OUR METHOD.
WHATTA YA MEAN?
YOU KNOW, LIKE... OUR STRATEGY. OUR APPROACH TO STUDYING.
LIAM AND I ALWAYS STUDY TOGETHER! WE'VE GOT IT DOWN TO A SCIENCE!
SCIENCE?
NEWS FLASH, GENIUSES: WE'RE SUPPOSED TO BE WORKING ON SOCIAL STUDIES!
WE MAY HAVE TO DUMB IT DOWN.
Peirce

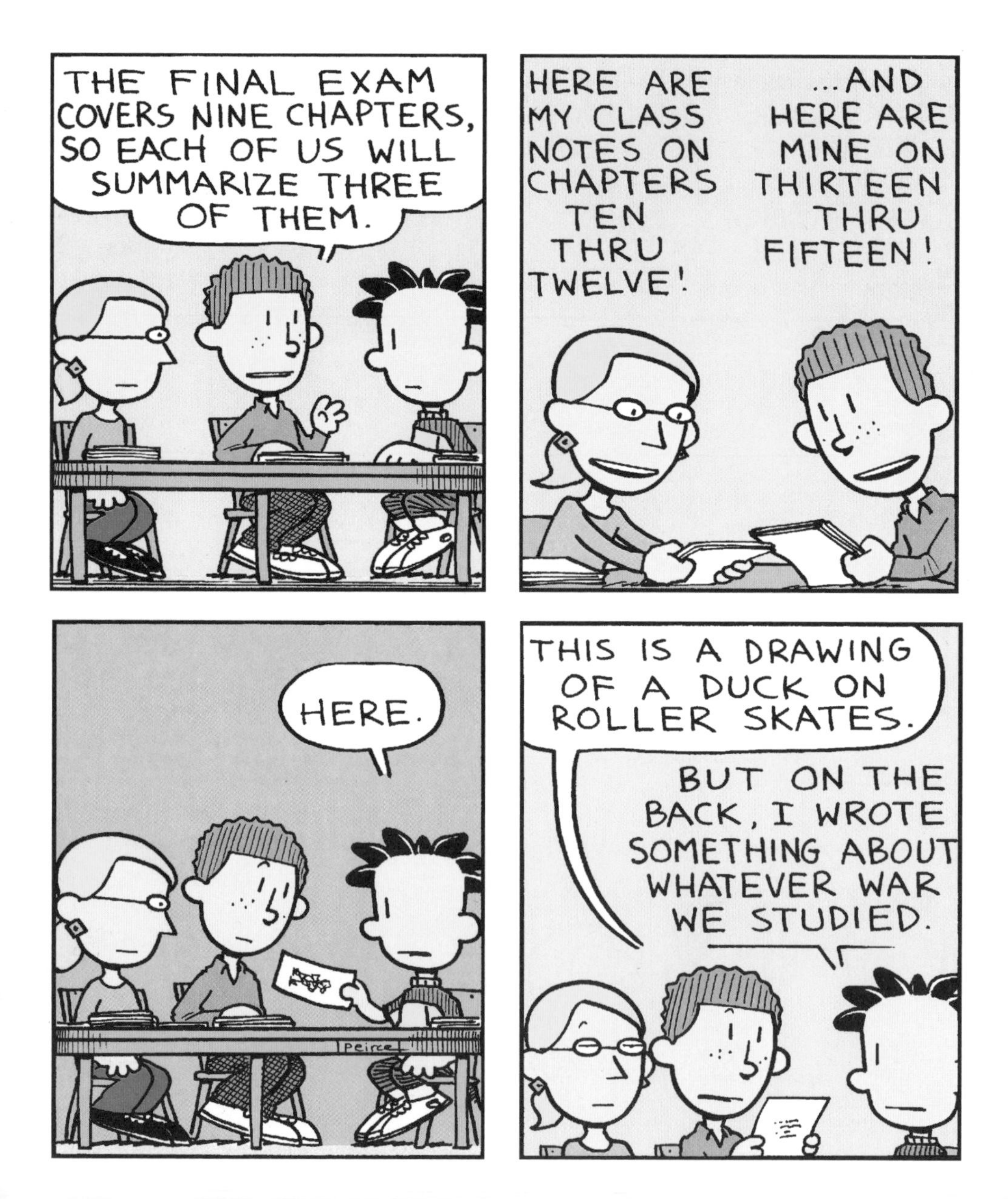
THE FINAL EXAM COVERS NINE CHAPTERS, SO EACH OF US WILL SUMMARIZE THREE OF THEM.
HERE ARE MY CLASS NOTES ON CHAPTERS TEN THRU TWELVE!
...AND HERE ARE MINE ON THIRTEEN THRU FIFTEEN!
HERE.
Peirce
THIS IS A DRAWING OF A DUCK ON ROLLER SKATES.
BUT ON THE BACK, I WROTE SOMETHING ABOUT WHATEVER WAR WE STUDIED.

...AND REMEMBER THAT TIME SHE HAD A PIECE OF COTTAGE CHEESE ON HER FACE FOR THE WHOLE DAY?
HA HA!

LISTENING TO HIS STORIES ABOUT MRS. GODFREY ISN'T HELP-ING US STUDY.
I KNOW, BUT... HE **IS** PRETTY FUNNY.

DON'T YOU SEE WHAT'S HAPPENING, ZOEY? HE'S DISRUPT-ING OUR PROCESS! HE'S POISONING OUR WHOLE APPROACH!

HE'S **TOXIC!**
YOU DON'T SMELL SO GREAT YOURSELF, LIAM.
Peirce

OKAY, LIAM, YOU CAN STOP WHINING THAT I'M NOT CONTRIBUTING ENOUGH TO YOUR LITTLE STUDY GROUP!
I **KNEW** I'D FINISHED THIS! I JUST HAD TO DIG IT OUT OF MY LOCKER, THAT'S ALL!
WHAT IS IT?
MY SUMMARY OF CHAPTER SIXTEEN!
"CHAPTER SIXTEEN IS JUST LIKE CHAPTER FIFTEEN, BUT WITH FEWER PICTURES."
WELL, ENOUGH WORK! HOW 'BOUT A SNACK BREAK?
Peirce

WAAH!
MIRANDA! HEY, WHAT'S WRONG?
SNIFFLE! I CAN'T REMEMBER WHERE I LEFT MY DOLLY!
AH-HA! NEVER FEAR, NATE IS HERE!
I'M GREAT AT FINDING STUFF!
SPITSY
OH HO! HERE IT IS!
ZING!
NOW I REMEMBER WHERE I LEFT HER!

GINA! HEY, I JUST HEARD! BETTER LUCK NEXT YEAR!
HUH?
I MEAN, BEING RUNNER-UP IS REALLY GOOD, BUT...
RUNNER-UP? DEE DEE, WHAT ARE YOU TALKING ABOUT?
OH! SORRY, I ASSUMED YOU KNEW!
KNEW ABOUT WHAT?
THE "STUDENT OF THE YEAR" AWARD!
GAWK!
peirce

YOU GOT THE "STUDENT OF THE YEAR" AWARD? YOU?
YUP!
YOU AND I WERE THE FINALISTS, AND THEY CHOSE ME!
BUT YOU'RE AN IDIOT! YOUR GRADES STINK!
IT'S NOT JUST GRADES! IT'S ABOUT BEING A GOOD CITIZEN!
WHA—? HOW ARE YOU A GOOD CITIZEN?
EARLIER TODAY, I RECYCLED A CAN!
IT'S TRUE. I SAW IT.
THIS IS NOT HAPPEN-ING!!
peirce

I JUST CAN'T BELIEVE THAT YOU, OF ALL PEOPLE, WON THE "STUDENT OF THE YEAR" AWARD!
I WANT DETAILS! WHEN DID THIS HAPPEN?
TODAY!
FOOSH!
... WHICH, BY THE WAY, IS PRANK DAY.
PUNK'D MUCH, GINA?
PEIRCE

YOU SHOULD'VE SEEN THE LOOK ON GINA'S FACE!
HA HA! SOUNDS LIKE A GREAT PRANK!
TOO BAD YOU DIDN'T HAVE TIME TO PLAY ANY PRANKS ON TEACHERS!
YAAAAH!
FIRE ANTS!! FIRE ANTS!!
WHO SAYS I DIDN'T?
Peirce

WHAT'S THIS? SOMEONE LEFT A CAKE ON MY DESK?
"HAVE A GREAT SUMMER, MRS. GODFREY." WELL, ISN'T THAT—
PLOOF!!
DID I JUST HEAR A "PLOOF"?
IT'S A DISTINCT POSSIBILITY.
PEIRCE

SOMEONE RELEASED A COLONY OF FIRE ANTS IN MR. STAPLES' CLASSROOM.
THAT'S AWFUL.
AND A BOOBY-TRAPPED CAKE WAS LEFT ON MRS. GODFREY'S DESK.
WOW. SORRY TO HEAR THAT.
PLEASE GIVE THEM MY BEST.
I HAVE A FEELING YOU DID THAT ALREADY.
HAVE A GOOD SUMMER!
Peirce

TEDDY! LISTEN TO WHAT TASHA WROTE IN MY YEARBOOK!
"NATE: YOU'RE A NICE KID."
TASHA THE HOTTIE THINKS I'M NICE!
TASHA? YEAH, SHE SIGNED MINE, TOO!
OH HO! WHAT DID SHE WRITE TO YOU, CHAD?
LET'S HEAR IT!
"DEAR CHAD: SECOND SEMESTER WAS SO FUN! I CAN'T BELIEVE WE DIDN'T KNOW EACH OTHER UNTIL WE DID THAT SCIENCE PROJECT TOGETHER!
"REMEMBER HOW HARD WE LAUGHED DURING THOSE TWO WEEKS? YOU ARE AN ABSOLUTE RIOT!
"WE HAVE TO SEE EACH OTHER THIS SUMMER! OTHERWISE I'LL MISS YOU TOO MUCH! WILL YOU VISIT ME AT MY FAMILY'S LAKE HOUSE?
"THANKS FOR BEING SUCH AN AWESOME FRIEND!
THAT'S SWEET, CHAD. GOOD FOR YOU.
"CONTINUED ON PAGE 37."
FLIP FLIP FLIP FLIP
BEHOLD THE POWER OF CHAD!
Peirce

THIS IS SO LAME.
THE YEARBOOK? I THINK IT'S GOOD!
THE YEARBOOK'S FINE, IT'S THE WAY PEOPLE SIGN IT THAT'S BAD! HALF THE KIDS WHO SIGNED MY YEARBOOK WROTE "HAVE A GOOD SUMMER"!
I MEAN, HOW ABOUT A LITTLE CREATIVITY? WHEN I SIGN SOME-ONE'S YEARBOOK, I PUT SOME EFFORT INTO IT!
LIKE THE PICTURE OF YOURSELF ON HORSE-BACK YOU DREW ON MY TITLE PAGE?
I CALL THAT "ADDED VALUE"!
Peirce

I THINK I GOT ALL THE TEACHERS TO SIGN MY YEARBOOK!
NOT ME. I'M MISSING MR. ROSA.
BY THE TIME I GOT TO HIS CLASS-ROOM, HE'D ALREADY LEFT.
BUT THAT'S OKAY! I CAN ALWAYS DROP IN ON HIM AT HIS SUMMER JOB!
HEY! YOU GAVE ME **CHOCOLATE** JIMMIES! I WANTED **RAINBOW** JIMMIES!
I'M TERRIBLY SORRY, SIR.
TIPS
SWEET

HI, MR. ROSA! WHAT'S NEW AT "SWEET LICKS"?
NOT MUCH. JUST DOING MY USUAL SUMMER GIG.
TIPS
SWEET
SCOOPING ICE CREAM FOR MINIMUM WAGE, DEALING WITH RUDE CUSTOMERS WHO CAN'T BE BOTHERED TO TREAT ME WITH RESP-
YEAH, COOL. HEY, CAN I GET TWO SCOOPS OF MAPLE WALNUT IN A SUGAR CONE?
TIPS
SWEE
DID I MENTION THE RUDE CUSTOMERS?
...AND ON A RELATED NOTE, I'D LIKE TO START A TAB.
TIPS
SWEE
Peirce

I GOTTA TELL YOU, MR. ROSA, YOU LOOK KINDA BEAT.
I AM.
UNDAE_4.50
IE CUP_3.95
ONSTER_5.00
WORKING AT AN ICE CREAM SHOP IS EXHAUSTING.
PEPPERMINT
REALLY? WHY?
WEET
OKAY, DAISIES OF TROOP 5!! WHO WANTS ICE CREAM??
WE DO!
IT JUST IS.
SUNDAE_4.50
IE CUP_3.95
Peirce

MMM! MAPLE WALNUT!
YUP. A SOLID, TRADITIONAL FLAVOR.
SWEE
...UNLIKE ALL THE **DESIGNER** FLAVORS PEOPLE EXPECT NOWADAYS.
LIKE WHAT?
WELL, LIKE–
SWEE
I'M TRYING NOT TO BE DEVASTATED BY THE FACT THAT YOU DON'T HAVE MANGO CHUTNEY SEA SALT ON YOUR MENU.
TRY HARDER.
pairce

MR. ROSA, WILL YOU SIGN MY YEARBOOK? THAT'S THE WHOLE REASON I CAME DOWN HERE!
REALLY?
UNDAE — 4.50
E CUP — 3.95
WELL, IF YOU MADE A SPECIAL TRIP ON MY ACCOUNT, THE LEAST I CAN DO IS GIVE YOU A SPECIAL SIGNATURE!
HERE YOU GO!
UH... THANKS.
4.50
3.95
5.00
5.00
4.50
SIGNING IN BUTTERSCOTCH SAUCE IS KIND OF COOL, I GUESS, BUT THESE PAGES WILL STICK TOGETHER FOREVER.
Peirce

SO LONG, DAD! I'M GOING TO TEDDY'S!
DID YOU CLEAN YOUR ROOM LIKE I ASKED?
WELL, I- KOFF!
KOFF! KOFF! KOFF! KOFF!
ARE YOU OKAY?
KOFF! KAFF! KAFF!
I'LL GET SOME WATER!
KOFF! KOFF! KOFF!
HERE! HERE!
KAFF! KAFF! KOFF! KOFF!
BETTER?
WHEW! YEAH. I THINK I SWALLOWED A BUG OR SOMETHING.
...BUT IT'S ALL GOOD NOW. SEE YA, DAD.
OKAY, BUD.
WELL, THAT WAS DRAMATI—
RED SOX
SO YOU JUST RANDOMLY STARTED COUGHING?
IT'S CALLED A DIVERSION.

WHAT ARE YOU DOING, FRANCIS?
PUTTING THIS BUMPER STICKER ON MY MOM'S CAR!
"MY CHILD IS AN HONOR ROLL STUDENT AT P.S. 38." OH, THAT IS SO OBNOXIOUS!
WHAT'S OBNOXIOUS ABOUT IT?
IT'S CONCEITED! YOU'D NEVER SEE ME PUTTING A STICKER LIKE THAT ON OUR CAR!
I'M TOO HUMBLE.
SO IS YOUR GRADE POINT AVERAGE!
PEIRCE

IT'S OBNOXIOUS, I'M TELLING YOU!
NO, IT **ISN'T**!
LET'S ASK CHAD!
CHAD, WHAT WOULD YOU THINK IF YOU SAW A BUMPER STICKER ON MY DAD'S CAR SAYING "MY CHILD IS AN HONOR ROLL STUDENT"?
I'D THINK YOUR SISTER MADE THE HONOR ROLL!
HA HA HA HA HA HA HA
THAT'S HARSH, CHAD.
Peirce

WHY ARE HONOR ROLL KIDS THE ONLY ONES WHO GET THEIR OWN BUMPER STICKERS?
PLENTY OF **OTHER** KIDS HAVE ACCOMPLISHMENTS THAT ARE JUST AS IMPRESSIVE AS GETTING STRAIGHT A'S!
HOW ABOUT A BUMPER STICKER FOR **ME**?
"MY CHILD IS REASON-ABLY GOOD AT TABLE FOOT-BALL"!
"MY CHILD CREATED SOME MEMORABLE GRAFFITI IN THE BOYS' BATHROOM"!
F
F
F
Peirce

THERE GOES ANOTHER CAR WITH A "MY KID'S ON THE HONOR ROLL" BUMPER STICKER!
THAT'S THE SIXTH ONE WE'VE SEEN IN THE PAST HOUR!
RIGHT! THAT MEANS MY MOTHER ISN'T THE ONLY PARENT WHO DOES IT!
NO, IT MEANS THAT HONOR ROLL STUDENTS ARE A DIME A DOZEN! ANYONE CAN MAKE THE HONOR ROLL!
THEN WHY HAVE YOU ONLY MADE IT ONE TIME?
HAVING PROVEN MY BRAINPOWER, I DECIDED I WAS READY FOR OTHER LIFE EXPERIENCES.
DETENTION ISN'T A LIFE EXPERIENCE.
Peirce

I MAY NOT BE ON THE HONOR ROLL, FRANCIS, BUT I'M JUST AS SMART AS YOU ARE!
YOU JUST SEEM SMARTER BECAUSE YOU KNOW A LOT OF STUFF!
GEE, AND I THOUGHT KNOWING STUFF WAS A GOOD THING.
KNOWLEDGE DOESN'T MAKE YOU SMART! IT'S HOW YOU USE YOUR KNOWLEDGE THAT COUNTS!
...SAID THE KID WHO INVENTED THE CHEEZ DOODLE SMOOTHIE.
AN IDEA WHOSE TIME HAS COME.
Peirce

I HAVE A QUESTION FOR YOU, DAD.
IF I GOT REALLY GOOD GRADES, WOULD YOU PUT A BUMPER STICKER ON OUR CAR SAYING "MY CHILD IS ON THE HONOR ROLL"?
THIS IS SUPPOSITIONAL, I ASSUME.
UH... WHAT DOES SUPPOSITIONAL MEAN?
IT MEANS YOUR REPORT CARD JUST ARRIVED.
OH, REALLY?
CLASSIFIED
METRO
Peirce

I'M TELLING YOU, IT'S A T. REX!
NO, IT'S A RACE CAR. SEE THE WHEELS?
TEDDY, IT'S **CLEARLY** A T. REX!
YOU'RE CRAZY. FRANCIS WILL SETTLE THIS.
SETTLE WHAT?
LOOK RIGHT UP THERE, AND TELL US WHAT YOU SEE.
WELL, IT'S OBVIOUSLY A CUMULUS CLOUD, AND MOST LIKELY A CUMULONIMB—
WHOA! **WHOA!**
WE DON'T NEED THE **SCIENTIFIC TERMINOLOGY,** DIPWAD! JUST TELL US WHAT YOU THINK THE CLOUD **LOOKS** LIKE!
RAIN.
WHAT A DRIP.
Peirce

OOH! LOOK!
WHAT?
THERE'S A NEWS TRUCK OVER THERE! LET'S GO SEE WHAT'S GOING ON! MAYBE WE CAN GET ON TV!
...AND MAYBE SOME FAMOUS DIRECTOR WILL SEE ME ON TV! AND MAYBE I'LL BECOME A STAR!
OR MAYBE THE NEWS TRUCK GUY IS JUST TAKING A DONUT BREAK.
IT'S A MUFFIN.
Peirce

ARE YOU HERE FOR A NEWS STORY?
SORT OF. WE'RE SHOOTING VIDEO OF THIS INTER-SECTION.

THE CITY'S THINKING OF TEARING IT UP AND PUTTING IN A TRAFFIC CIRCLE.
CARE TO... AHEM!... INTERVIEW A LOCAL RESIDENT?

NOT MY JOB. YOU WANT TO GET INTER-VIEWED, TALK TO THE CAMERAMAN. HE'S OVER THERE.

SCHOOL PICTURE GUY!
THAT'S "TV CAMERA GUY," KID.

SCHOOL PICTURE GUY, I DIDN'T KNOW YOU WORKED FOR CHANNEL 12 ACTION NEWS!
IT'S A NEW GIG, M'BOY!...
...AND THE TV STATION OBVIOUSLY VALUES MY SKILLS, BECAUSE THEY'VE GIVEN ME SUCH AN **IMPORTANT ASSIGNMENT**!
BUT... YOU'RE SHOOTING VIDEO OF A **STOP SIGN**.
YES, BUT WITH THE PROPER **ARTISTRY**, A PROJECT CAN BECOME A **MASTER-PIECE**!
THAT'S WHAT YOU SAID ABOUT "BATMAN V. SUPERMAN: DAWN OF JUSTICE."
QUIET ON THE SET, KID.
peirce

SO YOU'RE SHOOTING VIDEO OF THIS STREET?
TEN-FOUR, AMIGO.
12
NEW
WELL, ISN'T IT KIND OF EMPTY? IT WOULD BE MORE INTERESTING WITH A COUPLE PEDESTRIANS!
HMM! NOT A BAD IDEA, KID!
YOU TWO GO STROLL ALONG THE SIDEWALK! JUST ACT NATURAL! PRETEND IT'S JUST A NORMAL DAY!
WE'RE ROLLING IN THREE...TWO...
YOU'RE IN MY LIGHT.
SHOVE!
peirce

HOLD IT, DOODLEBUG! PUMP THE BRAKES!
THIS IS SUPPOSED TO BE AN EVERYDAY STREET SCENE! YOU'RE SUPPOSED TO BE A RANDOM PASSERBY!
WHY ARE YOU DANCING AROUND AND MUGGING FOR THE CAMERA LIKE A CRAZED BROADWAY WANNA-BE?
BECAUSE YOU TOLD HER TO BE HERSELF.
AND FYI, I'M A HOLLYWOOD WANNA-BE. JUST SAYIN'.
PEIRCE

SO WHEN WILL WE SEE OURSELVES ON CHANNEL 12 NEWS?
WELL, I CAN'T PROMISE ANYTHING.
CAN'T PROMISE ANYTHING? BUT YOU'RE THE **CAMERA GUY!**
THAT DOESN'T MEAN I GET TO MAKE DECISIONS.
OTHER PEOPLE AT THE STATION... UH... OUTRANK ME.
WHAT OTHER PEOPLE?
GET IN THE VAN, LARD BUTT.
PRETTY MUCH EVERYBODY.
Peirce

HOLY COW!
WHAT IS THAT, A DICTIONARY?
JUST SOME NOTES!
I REALIZED DURING THIS PAST YEAR THAT OUR SOCIAL STUDIES TEXTBOOK IS LAME!
IT'S OUT OF DATE, POORLY ORGANIZED, AND THE WRITING IS COMPLETELY LACKING IN SUBTLETY!
I DECIDED I COULD DO BETTER! I'M GOING TO WRITE MY OWN SOCIAL STUDIES TEXTBOOK!
I'VE ALREADY FINISHED THE CHAPTERS ON THE EARLY COLONIAL ERA AND THE EVENTS LEADING TO THE REVOLUTIONARY WAR!
IF I DO SAY SO MYSELF, MY ANALYSIS OF THE FIRST CONTINENTAL CONGRESS IS PARTICULARLY FASCINATING! I'LL READ YOU AN EXCERPT!
FLIP FLIP
AHEM! "JOHN ADAMS STEPPED OUT OF HIS CARRIAGE ON A HOT SEPTEMB"—
TSK! THIS BEACH USED TO BE SO CLEAN.
PEIRCE

BUT WHY MUSHT WE GO TO THE BEACH?
BECAUSE I SAY SO, PETER!
I'M THE BABYSITTER, AND IT'S MY JOB TO COME UP WITH FUN ACTIVITIES FOR YOU.
"FUN ACTIVITIESH"?
GETTING SHAND IN MY BATHING TRUNKSH ISHN'T A FUN ACTIVITY!!
NOBODY CALLS THEM BATHING TRUNKS, PETER.
ALREADY THERE'SH A GRIT FARM IN MY NETHER REGIONSH.
SKRITCH SKRITCH
Peirce

THE FIRST STEP IN ANY BEACH DAY, PETER, IS FINDING THE PERFECT SPOT!
AH! WHAT DO YOU THINK ABOUT **RIGHT HERE**?
STOP BLOCKING MY SUN, BRILLO HEAD, OR I'LL STUFF A CLAMSHELL UP YOUR NOSE.
LET'S KEEP LOOKING.
YOU NEVER SHAID THERE'D BE ENTERTAINMENT!
Peirce

THE SHUN IS TOO HOT.
SO GO GET WET!
BUT THE WATER ISH FREEZ-ING!
RIGHT! IT COOLS YOU OFF! THEN THE SUN WARMS YOU UP AGAIN!
YOU LIE IN THE SUN, YOU GET IN THE WATER... YOU LIE IN THE SUN, YOU GET IN THE WATER...ALL DAY LONG!
HOW INDESHCRIBABLY THRILLING.
IF YOU WANT TO SPICE THINGS UP, WE CAN COUNT SEAGULLS!
Peirce

HERE'S A CLASSIC BEACH ACTIVITY, PETER! BUILDING A SANDCASTLE!
A SHAND-CASHTLE?
WHAT DO WE DO WITH IT AFTER IT'SH DONE?
UH... NOTHING, REALLY.
WHAT HAPPENSH WHEN THE TIDE COMESH IN?
WELL... THEN IT'S GONE.
JUSHT LIKE THE LASHT FEW MINUTESH OF MY LIFE.
IT MIGHT BE TIME FOR A SNACK BREAK.
Peirce

LOOK, PETER! I SET UP A HORSESHOE PIT!
HORSHE-SHOESH? ISHN'T THAT DANGER-OUSH?
THEY'RE TOY HORSESHOES! THEY'RE MADE OF RUBBER SO NOBODY CAN GET—
ZING!
KLONK!
I'M BEGINNING TO QUESTION THAT WHOLE THING ABOUT HORSESHOES BEING GOOD LUCK.
I LIKE THISH BEACH!

TIME FOR MORE SUN-SCREEN, PETER. YOUR MOM TOLD ME TO RE-APPLY THIS STUFF EVERY HOUR.
IT SHMELLS FUNNY.
WE RAN OUT OF YOUR STUFF, SO I'M USING MINE.
WAIT, WHAT ARE THE INGRED-IENTSH?
SPLTT!
UH... ZINC OXIDE, BEESWAX, COCOA BUTTER...
I'M ALLERGIC TO COCOA BUTTER!!
5 MINUTES LATER...
Y'KNOW WHAT WOULD BE FUN? NOT MENTIONING THIS TO YOUR MOM.
FIRST AID STATI
CRIPESH.
peirce

DADDY! DADDY!
WHAT'S UP, PAL?
I SAW TWO HERMITS IN THE WOODS!
HERMITS. UH-HUH.
A BIG ONE AND A LITTLE ONE!
I KNEW THEY WERE HERMITS BECAUSE THEY LOOKED ALL TIRED AND DIRTY!
AND WHAT WERE THESE HERMITS DOING IN OUR BACKYARD?
WALKING AROUND! THE BIG ONE HAD A STICK, AND—
JIMMY, REMEMBER WHAT MOMMY AND I HAVE TOLD YOU ABOUT MAKING UP STORIES?
BUT DADDY!..
SON, THOSE WOODS ARE SO DENSE AND SWAMPY THAT NOBODY IN HIS RIGHT MIND WOULD—
WHAT TOWN ARE WE IN?
I TOLD YOU THIS WASN'T THE WAY BACK TO THE SEVENTH TEE.

WHAT DO YOU MEAN, YOU CAN'T MAKE IT? I'M HERE ALREADY! I BOUGHT MY TICKET AND EVERYTHING!
THANKS A LOT, TEDDY! NOW I HAVE TO PLAY BY MYSELF!
THERE'S NOTHING WORSE THAN PLAYING MINI GOLF ALONE!
OH, HO!
ACTUALLY, YES, THERE IS.
LOOKS, JENNY! NATE IS TO GOLFING, TOO!
Peirce

THIS WILL BEING **FUN**, NATE! ALL THE THREE OF US CAN MINI GOLFING **TOGETHER**!
NOT SO FAST, ARTUR!
IT NEVER WORKS WHEN A **SINGLE** PERSON HANGS OUT WITH A **COUPLE**! YOU GUYS ARE ON A **DATE**!
YOU'RE GOING TO BE ALL OVER EACH OTHER WITH THE BABY TALK AND THE PET NAMES AND ALL THAT JAZZ!
WHAT? NO! WE WOULD NEVER DO THAT!
...WOULD WE, CUDDLE CUB?
NEVER, SNOOKUMS!
UH-HUH.

HERE YOU GO. THREE PUTTERS.
THANK YOU.
AND WE HAVE EIGHT DIFFERENT BALL COLORS...
RED, PLEASE.
AND I WILL HAVE BLUE, BECAUSE BLUE IS COLOR OF JENNY'S EYES!
AND I'LL TAKE HAZEL, BECAUSE **HAZEL** IS THE COLOR OF **ARTUR'S** EYES!
WE DON'T HAVE HAZEL BALLS, KID.
THEN I'LL BE BLUE, TOO!
OH, BROTHER.
Peirce

HOKAY! HOLE NUMBER ONE!
WHO GETS TO GO FIRST?
E 1
I THINKS YOU SHOULD, JENNY!
NO, HONEY BUNNY, YOU SHOULD!
HOLE
NO, YOU SHOULD, BECAUSE YOU ARE SO SWEET.
BUT YOU'RE EVEN SWEETER!
NO, YOU ARE!
NO, YOU ARE!
YOU'RE BOTH SPECIAL. SOMEBODY HIT A STINKIN' BALL.
Peirce

I THINK I WILL BE NOT SO GOOD. I AM NOT EVER PLAY MINI GOLF BEFORE.
JUST GET IT CLOSE TO THE HOLE, ARTUR.
YES. CLOSE TO HOLE.
KLIK!
PLUNK!
IS ALSO OKAY TO PUT BALL **IN** HOLE, RIGHT?
NICE SHOT.
Peirce

ARTUR, YOU'RE AMAZING! I THOUGHT YOU SAID YOU'D NEVER PLAYED MINI GOLF BEFORE!
IS TRUE!
BUT YOU'RE PLAYING GREAT! YOU'RE MAKING ALL THESE AWESOME SHOTS!
YEAH, YOU'RE ACTUALLY WINNING RIGHT NOW! HA HA!
I AM? HA! THAT IS JUST TOTAL LUCKINESS!
KLIK!
YOUR BALL CAROMED OFF OF NATE'S AND WENT IN!
I MUST DESTROY HIM.
peirce

MISS IT.
KLIK!
HE'S ALREADY MADE FIFTEEN LUCKY SHOTS IN A ROW! HOW ABOUT HE MISSES ONE? JUST ONE!
HA! THAT'S MORE LIKE IT! THAT BALL HAS NO CHANCE!
OOP! WAIT! IT HIT A BUMP!
IT'S CURVING! OH, YOU MUST BE KIDDING ME!
IT CAN'T GO IN!... IT CAN'T POSSIBLY GO IN!
NO! NO! NO!
PLUNK!
NATE! ARE YOU SEE THAT?
I MISSED IT.
Peirce

I CAN'T BELIEVE ARTUR'S **BEATING** ME! I'VE NEVER SEEN SO MANY LUCKY SHOTS IN MY **LIFE**!
BUT I SHOULDN'T LET IT GET TO ME SO MUCH! IT'S ONLY A STUPID GAME OF MINI GOLF! WHY DO I EVEN **CARE**?
PLUNK!
I JUST DO.
Peirce

EIGHTEENTH HOLE! IF I MAKE THIS PUTT, I'LL **TIE** ARTUR AND SALVAGE AT LEAST A TINY SHRED OF DIGNITY!
KLIK!
GAAH!
I WAS LINING UP MY PUTT ON THE SEVEN-TEENTH, AND YOU BROKE MY CONCENTRATION.
SO MUCH FOR DIGNITY.
peirce

WELL, LOOKS LIKE YOU BEAT ME, ARTUR! THAT'S GREAT! HA HA! CONGRATULATIONS!
THANKS YOU, NATE!
CLUB
TURN
I DON'T MIND BEING RUNNER-UP! YOU CAN'T WIN 'EM ALL, Y'KNOW! I'M **FINE** WITH FINISHING SECOND!
UH... ACTUALLY, YOU FINISHED THIRD.
I KNEW I SHOULD HAVE KEPT SCORE MYSELF.
YOU ARE HURT MY HAND.
Peirce

DID YOU KIDS HAVE FUN?
YES! ABSOLUTE!
COME BACK SOON.
WE WILL!
ARE THOSE TEETH MARKS?
IT'S BEEN A TRYING DAY.
Peirce

HEY, DEE DEE.
WHERE'VE YOU BEEN? I WAS LOOKING FOR YOU!
I WAS MINI GOLFING WITH ARTUR AND JENNY.
OOH! WAS IT FUN?
OH, IT WAS GREAT! ARTUR DIDN'T MISS A PUTT ALL DAY!
HA! THAT'S SO ARTUR!
WOULD IT KILL HIM TO BE A LITTLE LESS ARTUR EVERY ONCE IN A WHILE?
HAVE YOU EVER NOTICED HOW GOOD HE IS AT EVERY-THING?
Peirce

AM I SENSING A LITTLE JEALOUSY OF ARTUR?
ME, JEALOUS OF ARTUR? NO! ABSOLUTELY NOT!
HE BEAT ME AT MINI GOLF, THAT'S ALL! I'M NOT JEALOUS! HE DESERVED IT! I'M HAPPY FOR HIM!
MM-HMM.
YOU'RE NOT BUYING IT.
I'M NOT BUYING IT!
Peirce

I DIDN'T EVEN LOOK AT THE SCHEDULE. WHO ARE WE PLAYING?
"JUST DESSERTS"
WAIT, **WHAT**? THERE'S **ANOTHER** TEAM IN THE LEAGUE SPONSORED BY A BAKERY?
YUP!
THEY'RE SUPPOSED TO BE GOOD, TOO.
HOW GOOD?
ASK CHAD! HE KEEPS NOTES ON ALL THE TEAMS!
CHAD! TELL ME EVERYTHING YOU KNOW ABOUT "JUST DESSERTS"!
AH!
THEY BEGAN AS A WEDDING CAKE BUSINESS, BUT FOUR YEARS AGO, THEY STARTED OFFERING A WIDE VARIETY OF TREATS!
THEY NOW MAKE CAKES, PIES, MUFFINS, CROISSANTS, BREADS, SCONES, AND ALL KINDS OF PASTRIES!
EVERYONE RAVES ABOUT THEIR ECLAIRS, BUT GIVE ME THEIR HONEY BUNS **ANY** DAY!
SWEET SCOUTING REPORT!
I JUST WANTED TO KNOW IF THEIR PITCHER HAS A GOOD CURVEBALL.

SO WE'VE ESTABLISHED THAT YOU'RE JEALOUS OF ARTUR...
WHOA, WHOA! WHAT'S THIS "ESTABLISHED" STUFF?
WE'VE "ESTABLISHED" NOTHING!
OKAY, THEN, LET'S SAY THAT IT APPEARS THAT YOU'RE JEALOUS OF HIM!
THAT'S RIDICULOUS, DEE DEE! WHY WOULD I BE JEALOUS OF ARTUR??
JUST BECAUSE HE'S THE LUCKIEST STINKIN' ████ IN THE UNIVERSE??
ISSUES MUCH?
Peirce

JUST BECAUSE I THINK ARTUR IS LUCKY, DEE DEE, THAT DOESN'T MEAN I'M JEALOUS OF HIM!
THEN WHAT DOES IT MEAN?
WELL, OBVIOUSLY IT MEANS THAT... THAT HE'S... UH...
IT'S... IT...
OKAY, LOOK: DURING SUMMER VACATION, YOU'RE NOT SUPPOSED TO ASK QUESTIONS I CAN'T ANSWER.
THAT'S YOUR SOCIAL STUDIES FACE!
Peirce

OKAY, I'LL ADMIT THAT ARTUR GETS ON MY NERVES... BUT NOT ALL THE TIME!
THERE ARE PLENTY OF TIMES I LIKE HIM JUST FINE! AND I'LL THINK: HEY, ARTUR'S NOT SO BAD!
...BUT THEN IF I SPEND TOO MUCH TIME WITH HIM, I GET SICK OF HIM! KNOW WHAT I MEAN?
SURE.
ARTUR IS THE PINEAPPLE LIFE SAVER OF YOUR FRIENDSHIP WORLD.
RIGHT. THEY'RE OKAY, BUT WHO WANTS A WHOLE ROLL OF 'EM?
Peirce

DO YOU THINK YOU'RE JEALOUS OF ARTUR BECAUSE HE'S GOING OUT WITH JENNY?
NO, I'M OVER THE WHOLE JENNY THING.
IT JUST TICKS ME OFF THAT ARTUR IS A TINY BIT BETTER THAN I AM AT SO MUCH STUFF.
HE DRAWS BETTER... HE SINGS BETTER... HE PLAYS CHESS BETTER... IT'S SO **AGGRAVATING**!
GOOD THING HE CAN'T COMPETE WITH MY SMOLDERING SEX APPEAL, OR I MIGHT REALLY HATE HIM.
UH-HUH.
Peirce

LISTEN, NATE, I DON'T THINK IT'S A BIG DEAL THAT YOU'RE JEALOUS OF ARTUR EVERY SO OFTEN!
WE ALL HAVE AN ARTUR IN OUR LIVES: SOMEONE WE LIKE WELL ENOUGH, BUT WHO WE ALSO FIND ANNOYING!
REALLY? WHO'S YOURS?
SHELLY OSTERTAG.
WHAT? BUT SHELLY'S SO NICE!
I KNOW I KNOW I KNOW I KNOW!!

I'M GOING TO TEST YOUR THEORY THAT EVERYBODY HAS AN ARTUR IN THEIR LIVES!
CHAD! THINK OF SOMEONE YOU SORT OF LIKE, BUT ALSO FIND KIND OF ANNOYING!
HMM.
MATT DAMON!
NO, I MEAN SOMEONE WHO'S NOT FAMOUS.
BEN AFFLECK!
Peirce

AW. THERE'S A SEAGULL OVER THERE WITH ONLY ONE LEG. THAT'S SAD.
SEE HOW HE CAN'T KEEP UP WITH THE OTHER GULLS WHEN THEY RUN ALONG THE SAND? POOR GUY. HE'S REALLY STRUGGLING.
BUT I'D TRADE PLACES WITH HIM. I'D DO IT IN A **SECOND**.
CUE OVER-THE-TOP ANTI-SCHOOL RANT.
...BECAUSE **HE** DOESN'T HAVE SOCIAL STUDIES WITH MRS. GODFREY!!
Peirce

DAD, I'M NOT GOING BACK TO SCHOOL NEXT WEEK. I'M TAKING A "GAP YEAR."
KIDS USUALLY DO THAT BETWEEN HIGH SCHOOL AND COLLEGE, BUT HEY—WHY WAIT, AM I RIGHT? WHY WAIT?
SPEAKING OF GAPS...
peirce

HEY, DAD, CAN WE TALK ABOUT MY "GAP YEAR" IDEA?
POKE!
!
THAT'S THE FIRST TIME THE EDITORIAL PAGE EVER GAVE ME THE HAIRY EYEBALL.
Peirce

I PROPOSED THE IDEA OF A "GAP YEAR" TO MY DAD, AND HE TOTALLY SHUT ME DOWN!
ALL I WAS TRYING TO TELL HIM WAS THAT I DESERVE A **BREAK** FROM THE DRUDGERY OF **SCHOOL**!
WHAT DO YOU CALL THE LAST TWO MONTHS?
THAT'S JUST THE RESPONSE YOU'D EXPECT FROM SOMEBODY WHO WENT SHOPPING FOR 3-RING BINDERS BACK IN JULY.
Peirce

SO YOU'RE DESPERATE NOT TO GO BACK TO SCHOOL, AND YOUR DAD WON'T LET YOU TAKE A "GAP YEAR."
RIGHT.
WHAT ABOUT HOMESCHOOLING?
HI, KIDS!
PLINK!
PLONK!
I'M DESPERATE, NOT INSANE.
Peirce

WHERE ARE YOU GOING, DEE DEE?
CLOTHES SHOPPING!
YOU'VE GOT TO HAVE JUST THE RIGHT "LOOK" ON THE FIRST DAY OF SCHOOL!
WHAT ARE **YOU** GOING TO WEAR?
AN EXPRESSION OF PROFOUND DISGUST.
I'LL WEAR ANYTHING, AS LONG AS MY UNDIES ARE LOOSE AND BREEZY!
Peirce

"DOG LEFT AT CAMPSITE WALKS 1,000 MILES HOME." WOW.
LET'S SEE IF **YOU** HAVE A SENSE OF DIRECTION THAT GOOD, SPITSY!
WURF?
HOLD STILL! I'M GOING TO BLINDFOLD YOU!
...AND NOW WE'LL TAKE A LONG WALK...
? ? ?
...UNTIL WE END UP SOMEWHERE...
...WE'VE **NEVER BEEN** BEFORE!
WROFF!
OKAY, SPITSY! SHOW ME WHAT YOU CAN DO!...
GET US HOME!
ZIP!
TUG TUG
...AND AFTER YOU PASS THE GAS STATION, TAKE YOUR SECOND LEFT.
OH, BROTHER.
Peirce

Look for these books!

Big Nate is distributed internationally by Andrews McMeel Syndication.

Andrews McMeel Publishing
a division of Andrews McMeel Universal
1130 Walnut Street, Kansas City, Missouri 64106

www.andrewsmcmeel.com

20 21 22 23 24 SDB 10 9 8 7 6 5 4 3 2 1

ISBN: 978-1-5248-6065-3

Library of Congress Control Number: 2020933039

Made by:
King Yip (Dongguan) Printing & Packaging Factory Ltd.
Address and location of manufacturer:
Daning Administrative District, Humen Town
Dongguan Guangdong, China 523930
1st Printing—5/25/2020

These strips appeared in newspapers from
February 29, 2016, through September 4, 2016.

Big Nate can be viewed on the Internet at
www.gocomics.com/big_nate.

Join Max on a new quest!